W9-CYG-725

For Twinky, Kesah, Quillie and Miss T
(beach bunnies every one)

Text and illustrations copyright © 1995 Jennifer Selby

All rights reserved. No part of this publication may be reproduced or transmitted in any form
or by any means, electronic or mechanical, including photocopy, recording, or any information
storage and retrieval system, without permission in writing from the publisher.

Requests for permission to make copies of any part of the work should be mailed to:
Permissions Department, Harcourt Brace & Company, 6277 Sea Harbor Drive,
Orlando, Florida 32887-6777.

First published 1995 by ABC, All Books for Children,
a division of The All Children's Company Ltd., London

First U.S. edition 1996

Library of Congress Cataloging-in-Publication Data
Selby, Jennifer
Beach bunny/Jennifer Selby.
p.   cm.
Summary: Because of careful preparation, Harold the bunny enjoys an
active morning at the beach, but the outing is almost ruined when he thinks
that he forgot to prepare for lunch.
ISBN 0-15-200840-3
[1. Rabbits—Fiction. 2. Beaches—Fiction.] I. Title.
PZ7.S45665Be   1996
[E]—dc20   95-10685

A B C D E

Printed in Hong Kong

Beach Bunny

JENNIFER SELBY

HARCOURT BRACE & COMPANY

San Diego   New York   London

One sticky summer day, Harold's mother said,
"Whew! I do believe today is a beach day."
Harold sat up. He had to get busy. Harold
liked going to the beach, and Harold liked
being prepared.

First he got his swim trunks. Then he found his waterproof watch and a beach ball. By the time he was finished collecting everything he needed, this is what he had:

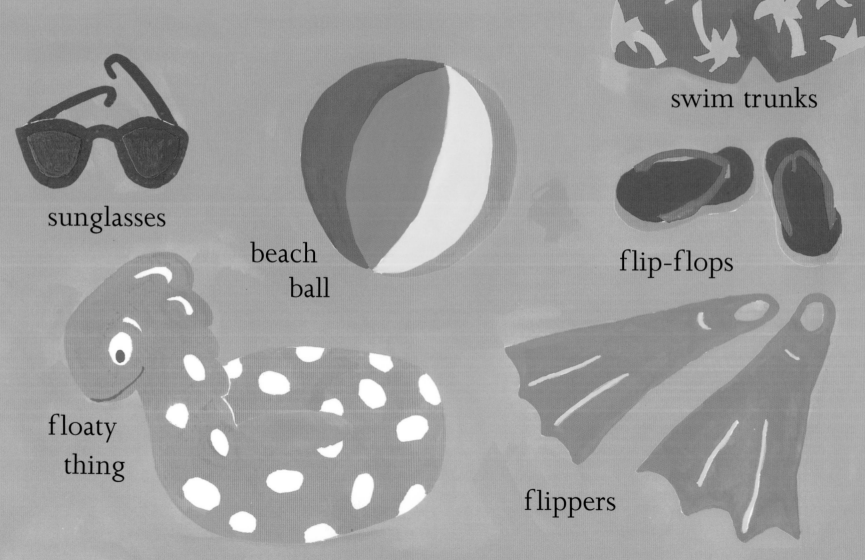

swim trunks

sunglasses

beach ball

flip-flops

floaty thing

flippers

goggles

suntan lotion

pail

net

shovel

fishing pole

sun hat

waterproof watch

snorkel and mask

fishing hat

"Ready?" asked Harold's mother. "Ready," said Harold. He put everything in his wagon, except his flip-flops (which he put on), and off they went.

When they got to the beach, Harold's mother put suntan lotion on Harold, spread out the beach blanket, and put up the umbrella.

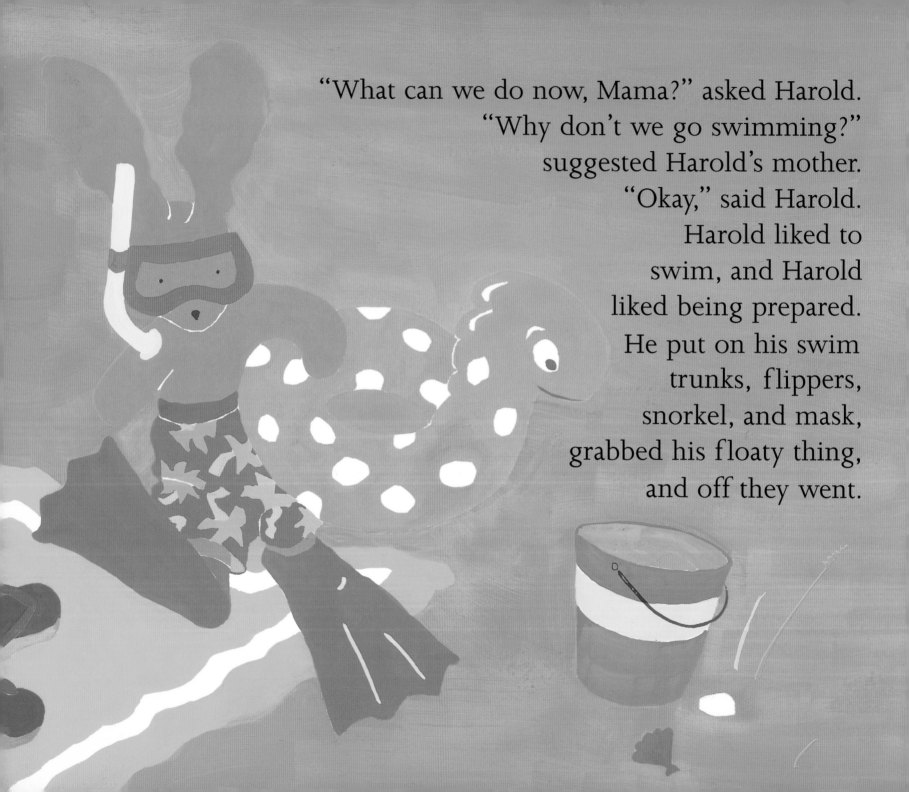

"What can we do now, Mama?" asked Harold. "Why don't we go swimming?" suggested Harold's mother. "Okay," said Harold. Harold liked to swim, and Harold liked being prepared. He put on his swim trunks, flippers, snorkel, and mask, grabbed his floaty thing, and off they went.

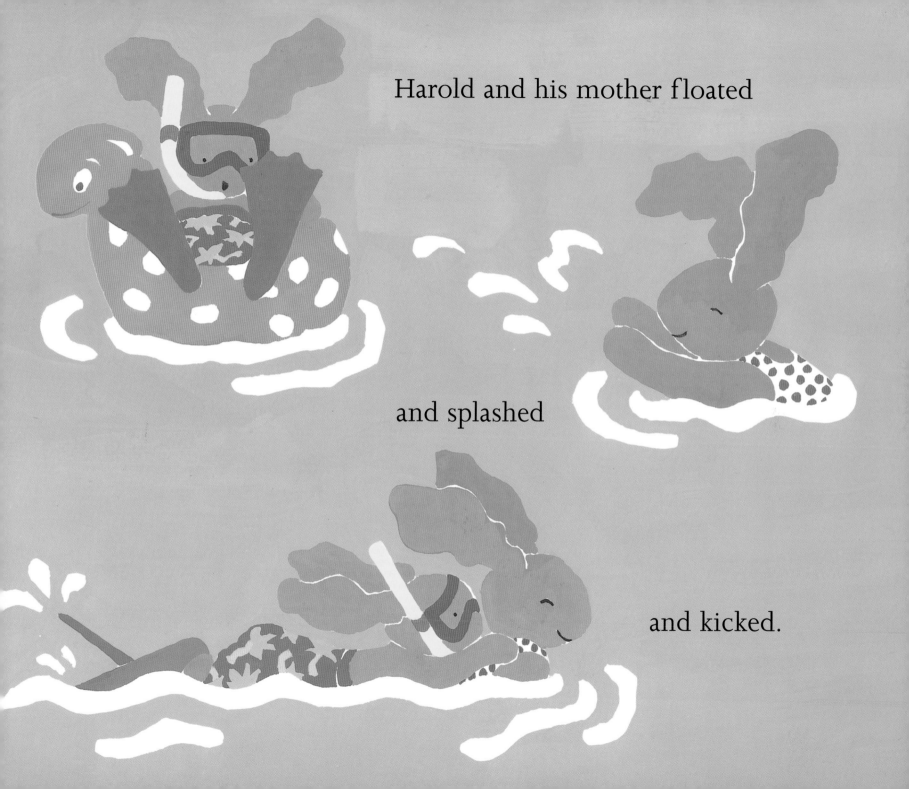

Harold and his mother floated

and splashed

and kicked.

Then a fish looked at Harold. Harold looked at the fish and decided he was too tired to swim anymore.

"What can I do now, Mama?"
asked Harold.
"Why don't you see if you
can find some seashells?"
suggested his mother.

"Okay," said Harold.
Harold liked looking for
shells, and Harold liked being
prepared. He put on his sunglasses,
sun hat, and waterproof watch (so he
would know when it was time for lunch),
grabbed his pail and shovel, and off he went.

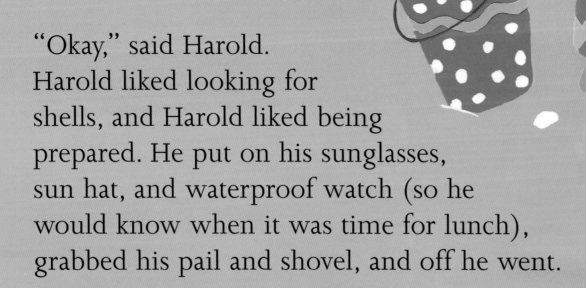

He found a big pink shell,

a shiny white shell,

and a curly
yellow shell.

Then a blue shell
with somebody
in it found him.

Harold decided
it was time to see
how his mother was.

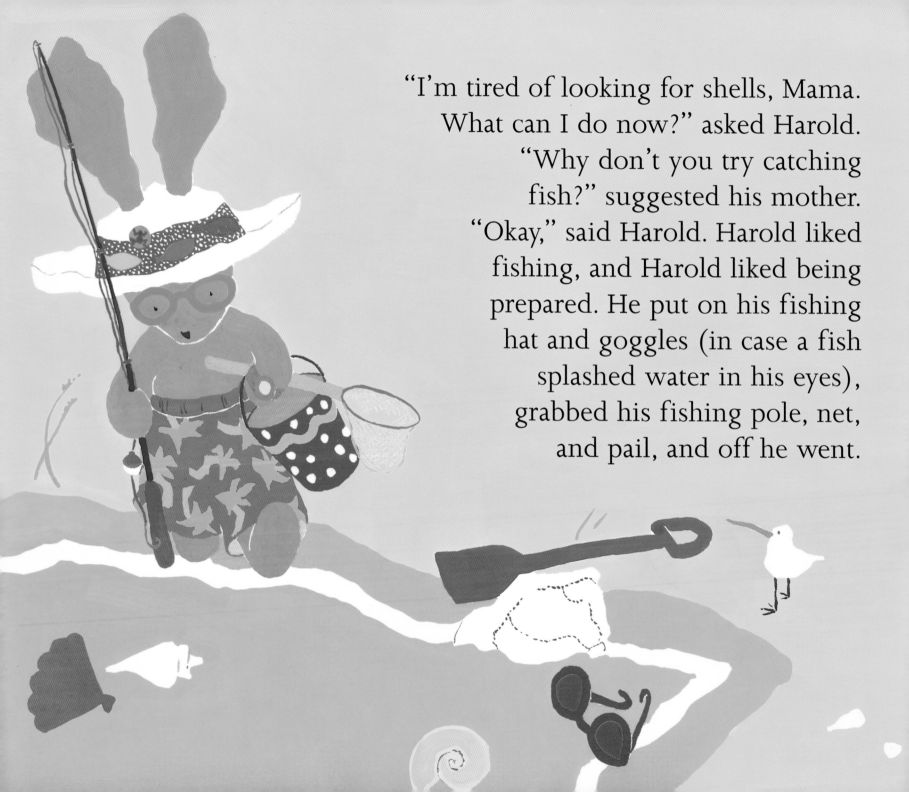

"I'm tired of looking for shells, Mama. What can I do now?" asked Harold. "Why don't you try catching fish?" suggested his mother. "Okay," said Harold. Harold liked fishing, and Harold liked being prepared. He put on his fishing hat and goggles (in case a fish splashed water in his eyes), grabbed his fishing pole, net, and pail, and off he went.

He caught a wriggly blue fish,

a polka-dotted fish,

and a black-and-orange striped fish.

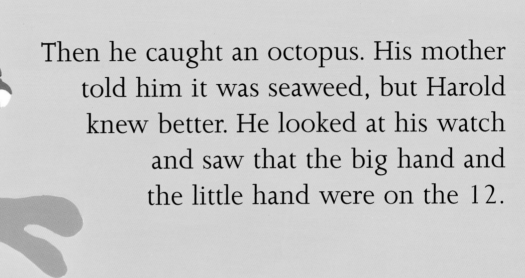

Then he caught an octopus. His mother told him it was seaweed, but Harold knew better. He looked at his watch and saw that the big hand and the little hand were on the 12.

"Mama, it's lunchtime," Harold announced.

"Okay," said Harold's mother. Harold's mother liked lunch, and Harold's mother liked being prepared. She opened the picnic basket. This is what was in it:

juice boxes

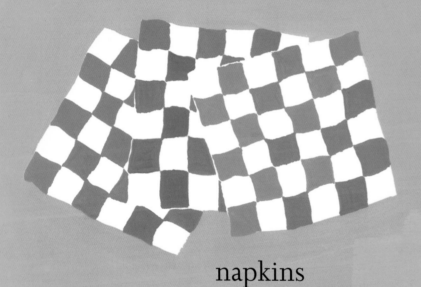

napkins

plastic plates

salt and pepper

raw carrots

pickled
carrots

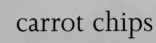

carrot chips

two
forks

carrot cupcakes

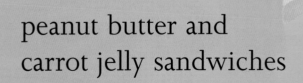

peanut butter and
carrot jelly sandwiches

carrot-raisin salad

"Ready?" asked Harold's mother.
Harold looked at his feet.
"What's the matter?" asked his mother.
A tear rolled down Harold's cheek.

"Mama," he said quietly, "I'm not ready.
I looked through everything I brought
to the beach, and I didn't bring
anything for lunch. I guess I'm
not a very good beach bunny."

"Harold," said his mother,
"let me look at your teeth."

Harold stopped crying. He opened
his mouth wide.
"Harold," said his mother, "you *are*
a good beach bunny. You brought
your rabbit teeth with you, and
that's all you need to be ready
for lunch."

"Oh, good!" said Harold.

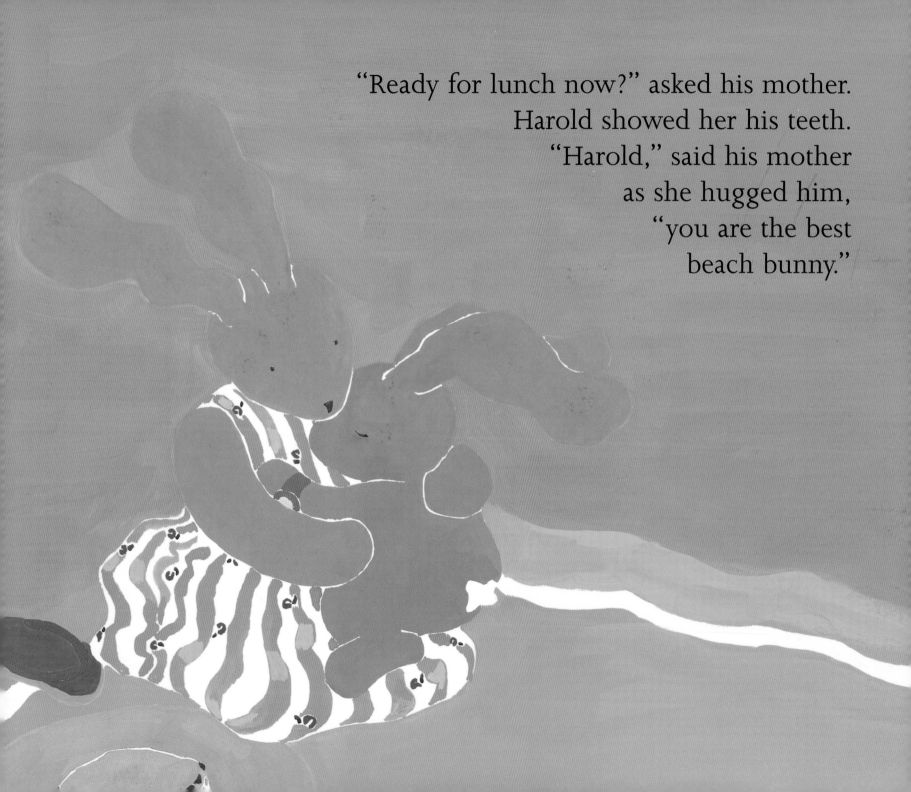

"Ready for lunch now?" asked his mother.
Harold showed her his teeth.
"Harold," said his mother
as she hugged him,
"you are the best
beach bunny."